PREHISTORIC PINKERTON

STEVEN KELLOGG

DIAL BOOKS FOR YOUNG READERS

NEW YORK

Published by Dial Books for Young Readers
A division of Penguin Putnam Inc.
345 Hudson Street
New York, New York 10014
Copyright © 1987 by Steven Kellogg
All rights reserved
Typography by Jane Byers Bierhorst
Printed in Hong Kong on acid-free paper
1   3   5   7   9   10   8   6   4   2

Library of Congress Cataloging-in-Publication Data
Kellogg, Steven.
Prehistoric Pinkerton.
Summary: Pinkerton's natural canine urge to chew on things while teething
coincides with a chaotic visit to the museum's collection of dinosaur bones.
[1. Dogs—Fiction. 2. Museums—Fiction. 3. Fossils—Fiction.] I. Title.
PZ7.K292Pr 1987   [E]   86-2201
ISBN 0-8037-2725-9

For Zachary Parkinson Porter
with love and cheers

Hi, Pinkerton, did you know that scientists have found the bones of giant dinosaurs that lived around here millions of years ago?

They think that dinosaurs are the ancestors of today's animals.

Maybe your great grandmother was a stegosaurus!

Billy Barret and I were going to wear this stegosaurus suit to the museum this afternoon as part of our class Dinosaur Day Pageant, but now he's sick and can't go.

Pinkerton, why are you eating the broom?

Something's wrong with Pinkerton. He just ate thirteen pencils and a broom, and now he's chewing on my bedpost.

The book says that he has begun the teething process, and that he will experience a strong urge to chew until he loses his puppy teeth.

I bet Pinkerton would love to chew gum.

The book suggests that Pinkerton chew on something hard,
like a rawhide bone.

Right now he's chewing on a tree in Mr. Arno's yard.

I'm sorry, Mr. Arno. Great Dane puppies can be a real problem. But we'll get Pinkerton through this stage with an order of rawhide bones.

That's not a Great Dane puppy, it's a giant beaver!
Keep that monster off my property!

Oh, dear. I'd forgotten that your piano
teacher was coming today.

I'll begin by showing you the new practice drills.

This instrument needs tuning. Its tones are quite unstable.

Excuse me, Professor, but I think that the problem is being caused by Pinkerton.

I feel faint!

I'm going to drive the professor home. When you leave for the museum make sure that Pinkerton has one of these rawhide bones to chew so he doesn't destroy the house!

I hope you'll feel better soon, Professor.

Yikes! There's no way I can leave you here alone. I'll have to hide you in the stegosaurus costume and take you to the museum.

Now remember, Pinkerton. It's important for you to keep quiet and behave so that everyone will think there are two kids in this costume.

I love you too, Pinkerton.

Class, it's an honor to introduce our guide,
Dr. Zandorfosaurus, the director of the museum
and an expert on prehistoric life.

I adore dinosaurs, and I have devoted my entire life to collecting their bones.

I'm particularly proud of this display, which contains some of the world's rarest fangs and molars.

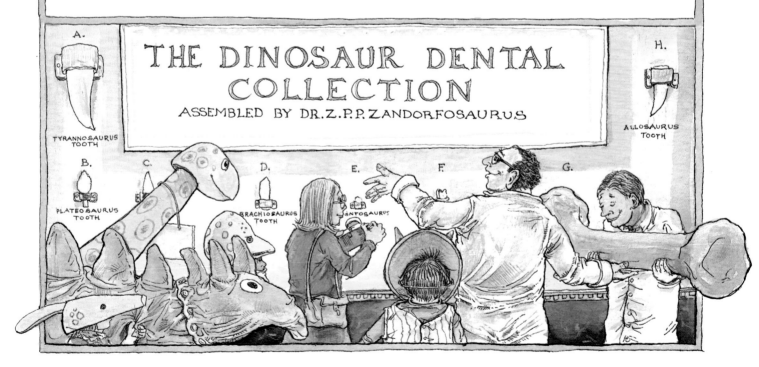

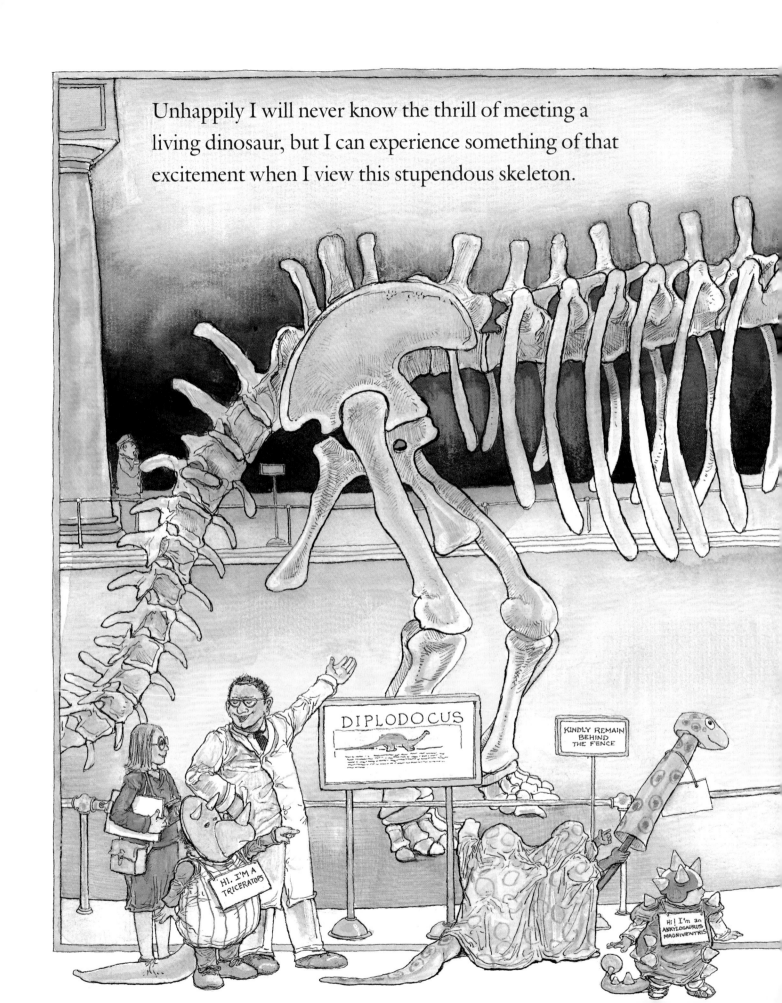

Pinkerton! Come back!

What are those children doing? No one is permitted to approach the skeleton!

Merciful heavens! It's a dog! Mobilize the staff!
Call the guards! Alert the pound!

Surround the mongrel! He's stealing a priceless bone!

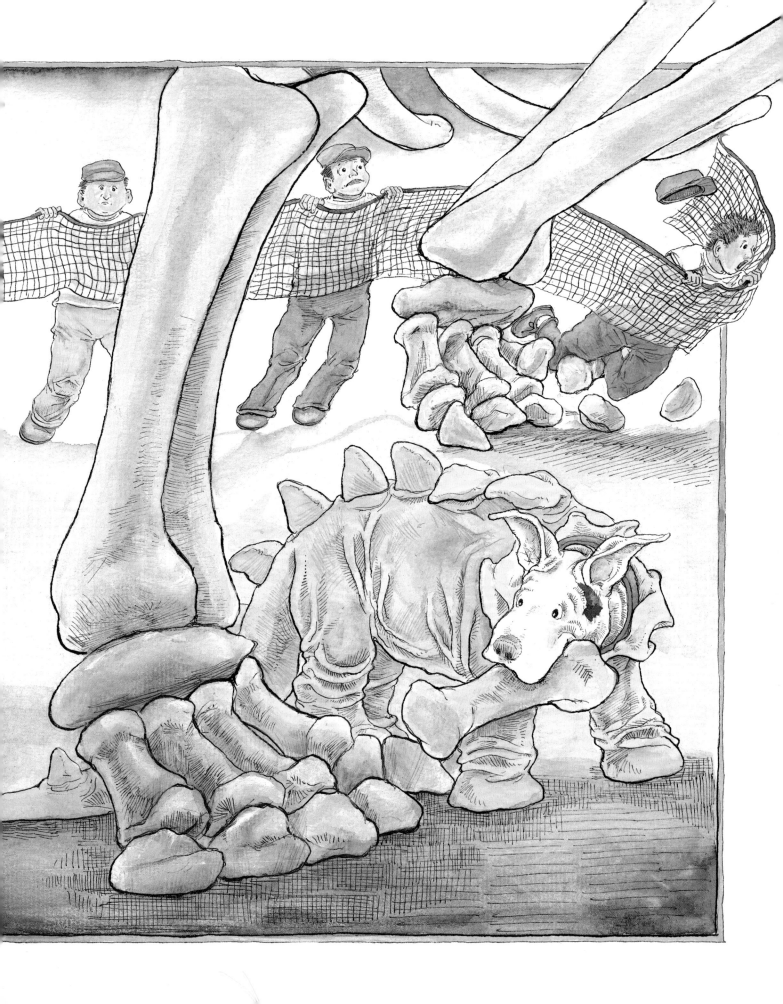

Pinkerton can't help what he's doing!
He grabbed that bone because he's teething!

Look! His puppy teeth are coming out!
The teething process is over!

Pinkerton and I would like to donate a tooth
to your Dinosaur Dental Collection.

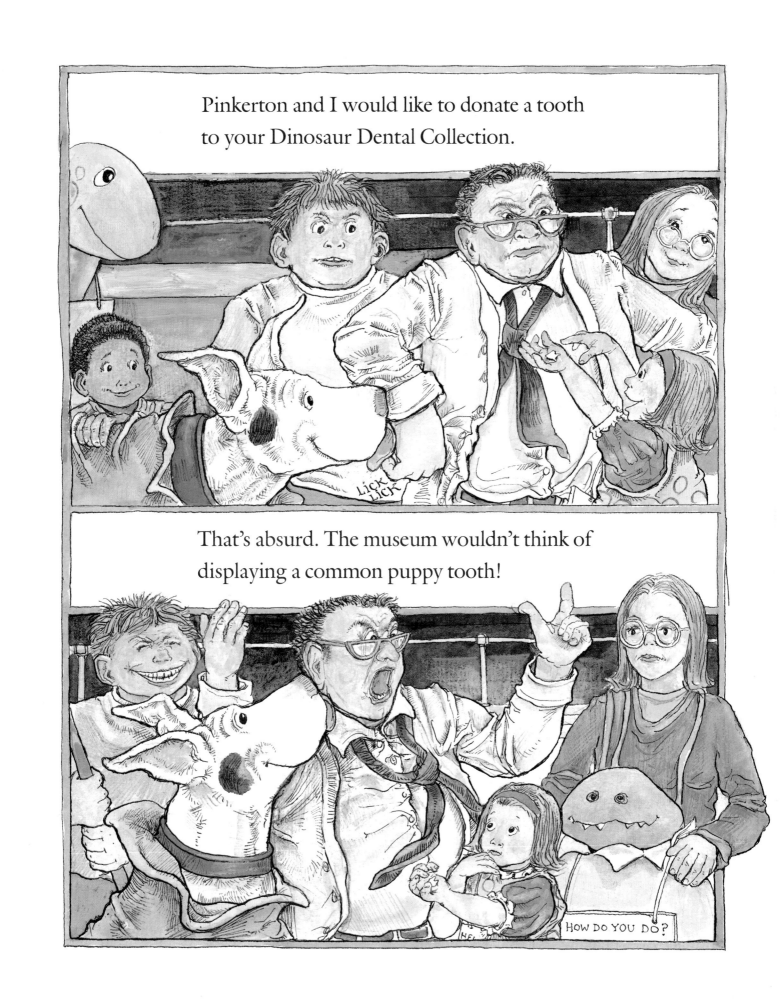

That's absurd. The museum wouldn't think of
displaying a common puppy tooth!

But Pinkerton's great great great great great great great
great great great great great great great great great great
great great great great great great great great great great
great great great great grandmother may have been a stegosaurus.

And meeting Pinkerton is probably the closest you will ever come to the thrill of experiencing a living dinosaur.

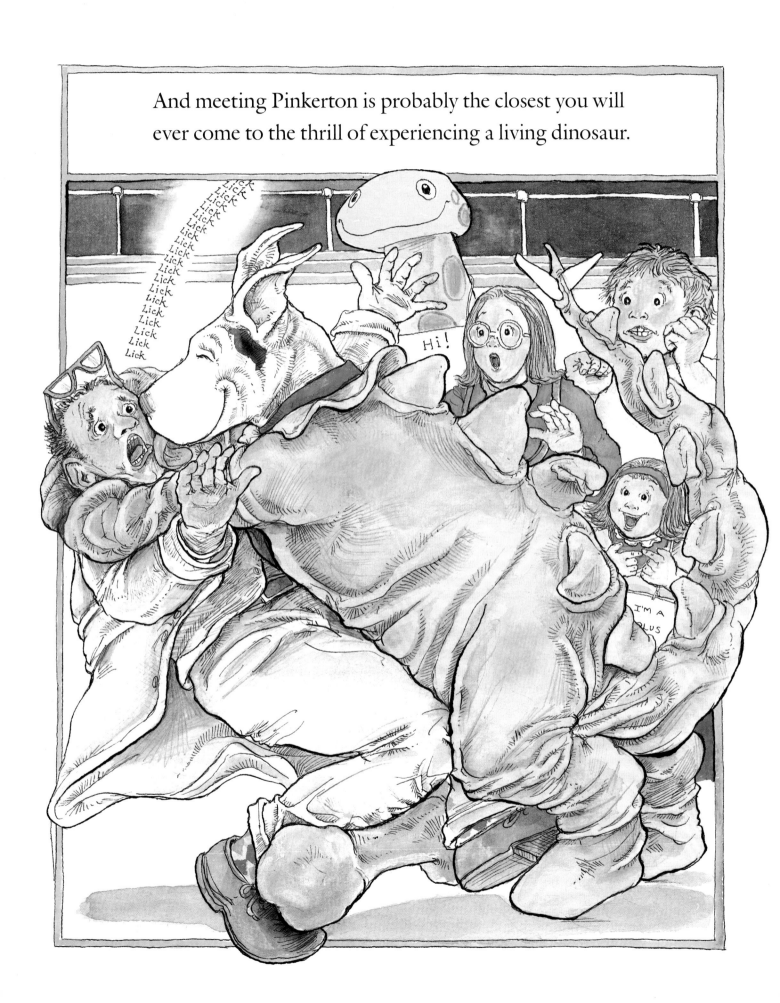

And besides, Pinkerton is a lot friendlier.